INSPIRING STORIES FOR

AMAZING BOYS

A Collection of Motivational Tales about Courage,

Perseverance, Problem-Solving and Friendship

Michelle Weiss

CONTENTS

JOIN OUR FACEBOOK GROUP!

If you want to:

- Discover the **latest releases**
- Be offered the possibility of **reading** every e-book (and for some lucky ones, the paperback!) **in advance for free**
- Share discussions with other members about the adventures and lessons your kids have found in our books
- **Learn about our books in progress** before anyone else, including illustrations, book covers, excerpts and more
- Receive some **free gifts**

And so much more!

Then join our Facebook community for exclusive access and fun surprises!

Scan this QR code to enter our group!

YOUR FREE GIFTS

As a way of saying thank you for your purchase, I'd like to offer you these two GIFTS, which I hope your child can enjoy!

To get access, go to the link or scan the QR:

https://michellebooks.com/free-gift

- The Amazing Coloring Book will set your little boy's creativity free!
- The Gratitude Journal will make him realize just how amazing his life truly is!

INTRODUCTION

What if I told you, I could show you someone truly incredible? Well then, run as fast as you can. Find a mirror and look straight into it.

Yes, it's you!

You ARE incredible!

Yes, you heard that correctly! There's something clearly special about you. Something that makes you shine brighter than a star. No one, and I mean NO ONE, can ever be like you. You are unique. You are extraordinary. And that should make you feel proud of yourself.

Do you know what's even cooler? You can show everyone just how remarkable you are! You can light up a room with your smile. With your gentle heart, you can make a thousand friends. When you're yourself, you make magic happen.

Now, here's a little secret: Sometimes, shining like a star can be hard. Life can be difficult. But you know what? Even grown-ups face tough times! Just know that there's always a solution waiting to be found. And you know who finds those solutions? The ones who are patient and never give up – just like you!

You're not alone when you feel life is hard. In this book, you'll meet a bunch of new friends like you. They too sometimes find things a bit tricky. Some of them aren't good at making friends. Others feel a little shy. And some struggle with their grades. But you know what they do? They always face those challenges head-on.

As you read about them, you'll find new things too. Little treasures that you can use to become even more amazing. Each friend's story is like a magical treasure. And it's waiting for you to find and learn it.

Now I'm sure you're excited to meet all these new friends. But before I leave you, there's just one thing I want to say.

Always remember, dear boy, that I believe in you with all my heart. Keep being your wonderful self!

Your biggest fan,

Michelle

LIGHT THE LAMP

"Ryan, get a move on! You don't want to be late for the game!" Ryan's mom yelled up the stairs toward Ryan's room.

"Coming, Mom!" Ryan finished putting on his socks and grabbed his sneakers before running down the stairs. Ryan's hockey game was an hour from now, and he was energized and ready to play.

"We must make one stop on the way. Nikita needs a ride to the game."

Ryan stopped in his tracks. "What? Mom, you cannot give him a ride to the game! He hates me!" Ryan couldn't believe this was happening. He could feel the positive energy draining from his body, and his stomach tightened.

Nikita's mom and Ryan's mom worked at the school, and they became friends last year when Nikita and his mom moved into town. Nikita's mom was sweet and kind, not like Nikita. He was big, mean, and scary. No matter how hard he tried, Ryan had been unable to make friends with Nikita, despite being on the same hockey team for a half season, despite going to the same school, being the same age, and having the same awesome sport in common. Nikita refused to hang out with Ryan and told his mom he did not want to be friends. Nikita called Ryan names and made fun of his hockey skills. On the ice, Nikita was competitive and rough with Ryan.

Ryan's mom said Nikita was struggling to adjust to his new school. He was a big fish at his old school and was now a small fry. Whatever that meant.

"He does not hate you, honey," Ryan's mom said. "He is angry because he had to leave his school and friends behind to move here. Ryan, let's work together and help Nikita make friends. What do you say?"

"I want to get along with him, Mom. I would rather be friends with him because I see him everywhere I go. You don't understand. He won't let us be friends." Ryan was exhausted by the situation.

With Nikita on an opposing team this season, Ryan had come face-to-face with him in the locker room area before and after games and on the ice. Ryan and his teammates were always nice to Nikita and tried to talk with him about hockey or school, but Nikita wouldn't accept their kindness. He did not have friends on his own team.

As they pulled up to the house, Ryan saw Nikita sitting on the steps with his mother. Nikita was frowning and kicking his hockey bag with his foot.

Nikita's mom walked him to the car, and Ryan's stomach got tighter as Nikita got closer.

Nikita was taller than Ryan, and he had more muscle. Nikita was the biggest kid in school, and he looked even bigger when he put on his hockey equipment.

"Hey, Nikita. Ready for the game?" Ryan asked sheepishly.

"I am ready to watch you lose. That's for sure," Nikita grumbled as he looked out the window at his mother.

"Have a good game, honey." She kissed Nikita on the head. "Have a good game, Ryan."

"Thanks," Ryan replied and waved goodbye. Ryan wondered how such a mean boy came from such a nice woman.

Nikita stared hard out the window while Ryan tried to think of something to say. Before he could speak, his mother chimed in.

"There is no game next Saturday, not for either of you. The weather is getting nicer, and you two should ride bikes together. Or go to the park?" Ryan's mom looked back and forth from Ryan to Nikita.

"Do you have a bike, Nikita?" Ryan asked.

"Of course, I have a bike. I used to ride all the time with my friends back home. But we are not friends, and I'm not going to ride with you," Nikita replied nastily.

"I know some trails we could ride on," Ryan tried.

"Nope," Nikita stated firmly.

"I am sure you two could find something fun to do together. Nikita, I will let your mother know you will be coming over to our house on Saturday. I will feed you dinner also." Ryan looked at his mom and wondered if she would ever give up on the idea of him and Nikita being friends.

The rest of the car ride was silent.

On the ice, at the tail end of the third period, Ryan's team was down by one point. Ryan skated up center ice, head up, dribbling the puck side to side. His eyes scanned the area around him, looking for opportunities to pass the puck. The only thing Ryan could see was Nikita looming over the right side of the goal. Ryan's teammate Tomas was stuck behind Nikita, unable to break free and open himself for the pass. The team needed one more goal to win.

With no opportunity to the left of the goal, Ryan decided he would attempt to fake Nikita out. Faking out was something Ryan had been working on with his father. Ryan and his father loved to play hockey together. They played on the concrete floor in the garage, in the street, and throughout the house. All they needed were two sticks, a puck, and each other.

Nikita looked like a giant as Ryan skated directly at him. Ryan's knees felt weak. He was scared as Nikita skated faster toward him, and before he knew it, Nikita was inches from him, pushing his stick up in the air, forcing Ryan to lose control of the puck.

"Loser," Nikita laughed as he circled Ryan. Finally, the referee blew the whistle, and the players headed back to their bench.

"Good try, Ryan. Keep it up," Coach said.

"If I keep that up, we will lose for sure." Ryan sighed, disappointed in himself.

"Lean in and listen, kids." Coach grabbed his whiteboard, and the team gathered around.

"Ryan, I like that you tried to fake the other player out. I want you to do that again. I do not think he expects you to use the same move twice. Let's catch him by surprise."

"Tomas, I saw you trying your hardest to get out from behind that defenseman, Nick...Nikki. Whatever his name is."

"Nikita!" the whole team chimed in loudly.

"What I want you to do this time is, Tomas, when he blocks you, skate behind the goal. Come out on the left side. A fake out of your own. Nikita will not notice that you are no longer behind him because he will be focused on Ryan."

Coach continued, "Ryan, the fake out is that you will pass to Tomas instead of taking the shot yourself." Coach grinned from ear to ear, satisfied with his plan. Ryan and Tomas nodded in agreement with the plan as the rest of the team gave encouragement and patted them both on the helmet.

"It's worth a try, Tomas," Ryan said. "My dad says it is not about winning or losing, it's how you play the game. So, I'm going to play the best I can."

"Teamwork makes the dream work. That is what my dad says. But I still want to win." Tomas laughed and extended his gloved hand for a fist bump with Ryan. Returning the bump, Ryan laughed as he stepped back onto the ice.

Ryan wanted to celebrate the game-winning goal with Tomas. Tomas was a good friend and teammate, and he made Ryan feel good about himself. Ryan thought back to what Nikita said in the car about riding his bike with his friends. Ryan thought about how lonely he would be without Tomas and how lonely Nikita must feel without his friends.

On the ice, Ryan and Tomas worked together to execute the play as Coach had instructed. Ryan was able to fake Nikita out and pass the puck to Tomas. Tomas was able to sink the puck into the net. The team went wild when the red lamp behind the goal lit up. They had won by working together.

On the ride home, Ryan was excited about the win, smiling from ear to ear. Nikita looked unhappy as usual. Feeling good about the win and his friendship with his teammates, Ryan was determined to help Nikita make friends.

"We can eat your favorite food for supper on Saturday. What is your favorite food, Nikita?" Ryan asked.

Nikita hesitated. He looked at Ryan. He was not frowning anymore but not exactly smiling.

"Pepperoni pizza. I used to eat it with my friends all the time back home. I miss that." Nikita hung his head.

"Would you like it if I invited some of my teammates over for pizza? They all think you are a great hockey player, and I know they would like to get to know you more." Ryan waited, afraid that Nikita might not accept his offer.

"I would like that a lot. Eating pizza. And making new friends." At last, Nikita smiled. He held out his fist to Ryan for a fist bump.

"Sounds great, loser." Ryan returned the fist bump, and they both laughed heartily. Ryan smiled at his mom, proud of their work together to start this new friendship.

THE BIKE MAKER

Yuri hurried so he wouldn't have to pass Rusty, the meanest boy in the entire school. Yuri would ride his bike past Rusty each day, and Rusty would say mean things. Yuri ignored him and pedaled as fast as he could until he reached school.

"Hey, Yuri, where'd you get that piece of junk?" Rusty would shout. "Did you find that bike at the dump?" There was no end to Rusty's meanness. And it didn't stop once they reached school. Rusty would shoulder bump Yuri whenever he passed him in the hall.

One day, Rusty wasn't on the corner where he usually stood.

"Whew," Yuri said to his bike. "You won't get made fun of today."

Yuri safely reached school, and after putting his bike in the rack, he locked it. He was proud of his bicycle. It was a black bike with a red banana seat. It had silver metal petals and a silver kickstand.

He looked back at his bike as he opened the door. He couldn't wait for the day to be over so he could ride home without worrying about seeing Rusty. If Rusty wasn't on the corner, he probably wasn't at school.

And he wasn't.

The day was even better now that Rusty was absent. It was going to be the best sixth-grade day ever! Yuri was so happy. He hurried to the cafeteria to tell his friend Norah.

He found her sitting at their usual table.

"Why are you smiling like that, Yuri?" she asked. "Why are you so happy? Did you pass your math test?"

"Better than that," Yuri answered.

"Then what is it?"

"Oh, Norah, Rusty is absent today. I feel free! No bully to worry about."

"That's such good news, Yuri. But I hope he's not sick or hurt."

Yuri's smile faded. "Yeah, I thought of that. I just like not having to look over my shoulder all the time. I hope he's okay, though."

Norah nodded and took a bite of her sandwich.

Yuri knew she was right. No matter how badly Rusty treated him, wishing him harm wouldn't be right. Still, Yuri couldn't help feeling relieved that he could have a day without being bullied.

Norah and Yuri finished their lunches and walked to their music class. It was Yuri's favorite. He loved to sing and play the piano. His father worked hard to have the extra money for piano lessons.

Yuri felt so relaxed. He sang loud and proud. He went to his locker to put his books away when class ended. He put on his jacket and took the key to his bike lock out of the pocket.

"I'll see you tomorrow," Norah said as she passed him in the hall. "Maybe Rusty will be absent again."

Yuri smiled. "Maybe. We'll see. I'm just happy I got to enjoy today. See you tomorrow."

Yuri whistled as he walked to the bike rack. The air was warm, not too warm, just perfect for a slow bike ride home. He took a deep breath and rounded the corner to where his bike was waiting.

"Wh—what!" Yuri screamed. "Wh—wh—where's my bike?"

Yuri ran to the bike rack. His bike was gone.

He ran back inside the school and into the principal's office.

"Yuri, what's the matter?" the principal asked the crying boy. "Have a seat and tell me what happened."

"I don't want to sit. My bike is gone. It's gone!"

The principal stood. "I'm sure it's a mistake. Come, I'll walk with you to the bike rack."

"See, it's gone," Yuri cried as he pointed to where his bike once stood.

"Are you sure it was locked?" the principal asked.

"Pretty sure, sir. I don't think I forgot."

Yuri hung his head. His bike was gone. The principal took him back inside so he could call his mother to pick him up.

Yuri sobbed when his mother arrived. She hugged him and told him not to worry; he'd get another bike.

"I don't want another bike. I want that one. Dad made it for me."

"I know, son. And he will make you another. Now, come along. Let's go home and get you washed up for dinner."

Yuri wasn't hungry. He only wanted his bike.

"I'll make you another one just like it," his father said. "I'm sure I can find another banana seat."

Yuri looked at his father with a half-smile. No one would understand how much he wanted his bike back. The banana seat wasn't just any banana seat. It was given to him by his best friend, Jeff.

Yuri and Jeff had been friends since kindergarten. Jeff lived across the street from Yuri, and as they got older, they rode bikes together. Yuri admired Jeff's banana seat, and when Jeff had to move away to another city, he gave Yuri the seat.

"Take good care of it," Jeff had said as he hugged his friend goodbye.

It was a special seat, and Yuri knew his dad would never find another one.

Yuri's mother was clearing the dinner dishes when the doorbell rang. She opened the door to find Yuri's bike between Rusty and his mother.

"I am here to return your son's bicycle," Rusty's mother said. "And my son has something to say."

Rusty hung his head. "I'm sorry," he mumbled.

"Perhaps you need to say that to Yuri. Won't you come in? You can bring the bike in too. I'm going to put it in the kitchen. I'll be right back."

Yuri came down the stairs and was face to face with his worst nightmare—Rusty.

"What's he doing here, Mom?" Yuri asked.

Rusty's mother tugged his arm. "Don't you have something to say to Yuri?"

"Sorry I took your bike."

Yuri looked around. He didn't see his bike, so he was confused. Why was Rusty apologizing for taking his bike? He didn't bring it back.

"Yuri, go look in the kitchen," his mother said. "I think you'll be pleased."

Yuri ran to the kitchen and let out a screech. "My bike, my bike!" He ran back to the living room, where his mom, Rusty, and Rusty's mom sat.

"Thank you for bringing my bike back. But how did you take it? And why? And why do you bully me every day?"

Rusty's mother passed a stern look to her son. "You've been bullying Yuri? I think you need to explain yourself, and then we'll go home, and you can explain it to your father."

Rusty's eyes filled with tears, and he let out a whimper.

"I don't know why, Mom. I'm sorry. You and Dad can't afford to get me a bike. You said so yourself... because Dad's been sick and can't work. Yuri has a cool bike, and I guess I was jealous that he has a bike and friends. I don't have any friends."

Yuri walked over to Rusty and stood before him.

"You don't have friends because you scare everyone. You make us feel uncomfortable. You'd have lots of friends if you were nice."

"I'm sorry. I just wish I had a bike."

Yuri tapped Rusty on the shoulder. "Come with me," he urged.

The two boys went outside and walked to the large garage behind the house.

"Here, come on in," Yuri said. "I want you to meet my dad. He's known as the bike maker."

Rusty was surprised. "The bike maker?"

"Yes, my dad makes old bikes new again, and he donates them to kids who don't have bikes. Do you want my dad to make you a bike? You can pick the colors and the kind of seat you want. He'll do whatever you'd like."

"Really?" was all Rusty could say. He didn't understand how Yuri could be so nice to him after all he'd done. "Your dad will make me a bike?"

"I sure will, son," Yuri's dad said, and Rusty smiled ear to ear.

"I would really like that. Yuri, I'm going to cry. Are you going to tell everyone if I do?"

"No, it's okay to cry."

Rusty spent the next half hour picking out his bike. Yuri's dad promised to make it just the way he wanted it.

"Let's go back inside and tell our moms," Yuri said. "And by the way, how did you get my bike from the rack?"

"You didn't lock it," Rusty said. "I watched you from behind the tree. When you went inside, I took it and rode all day. I was going to bring it back, but I decided to keep it. That was stupid of me, I know. I didn't feel like going to school because my dad was sick all night. I just wanted to be alone. My mom doesn't know I skipped school yet. I guess I better tell her before the principal calls her tomorrow to ask why I wasn't there."

"It's okay, Rusty. I understand."

"You do? You aren't mad at me?"

"I'm not mad. But if you promise to stop bullying me, you can sit with Norah and me at lunch."

"Really?"

"Really."

"Let's shake on it," Rusty said and held out his hand.

The boys went inside to their waiting mothers.

"Meet my new friend Rusty," Yuri said proudly. "Dad is building him a custom bike, and when it's done, we'll ride to school together. And Rusty will sit with Norah and me at lunch every day."

"That's wonderful, dear," Yuri's mother said. "I'm happy you and Rusty can be friends. Let's go to the kitchen and celebrate with some ice cream. What do you say?"

Rusty noticed a piano in the family room as the foursome started for the kitchen.

"Wow! Who plays the piano? I've always wanted to play," he said excitedly.

"I play," Yuri said. "I take lessons. I can teach you if you'd like."

"Oh, boy, I sure would. You're the best friend ever, Yuri."

"Thanks, Rusty. I'm glad we are getting to know each other. Once you start being nice to everyone, you'll have a lot of friends. You'll see."

"Being nice makes everything better," Rusty said. "I'm not going to be mean to anyone ever again."

Three days later, Rusty's bike was ready, and together, he and Yuri rode to and from school, laughing and enjoying their new friendship.

YES, I'LL BE YOUR FRIEND

Toby sat in the school cafeteria alone. It was okay. He was used to it. You see, Toby was the only black student in the school. He didn't understand why no one would sit with him at lunch. They talked to him in class. They didn't pick on him or bully him. They just stayed away in the cafeteria.

Toby opened his lunchbox and took out his jelly sandwich. It was his favorite grape jelly on crustless bread. His mom took the crust off and made his sandwiches just how he liked them.

"Hey, Toby," Lizzy called to him halfway across the room. "How's your lunch?"

He didn't want to shout at her, so he smiled and nodded. "Why doesn't she just come over here to ask me?" he said under his breath. "She's kinda strange."

When the bell rang, Toby and his classmates lined up near the door, waiting for their teacher to come to get them.

Lizzy moved behind Toby.

"Hey, Toby, can I touch your hair?"

"Sure," he answered.

Lizzy liked to touch Toby's hair. She liked the texture and would often stand behind him in the lunch line so she could feel it.

Toby didn't mind. Sometimes the other kids would ask too. Toby knew his hair was different from his schoolmates, and that was okay. He liked who he was, and he enjoyed learning about his heritage. His mom told him always to be proud of who he was. His only wish was that he didn't have to sit alone at lunch.

Toby didn't say anything to his mom. He didn't want to worry her, and he didn't want his classmates to think he was whiny. He knew his mom would march down to the school to find out why her son was sitting alone in the cafeteria. Toby didn't want that at all. It wouldn't be cool.

He was afraid, too, that his mom would think it was because of his skin color. Toby knew better. That wasn't it. Still, he couldn't figure out why no one wanted to sit with or near him.

"Hey, Tobes," Josh called out from the front of the line. "Do you want to play with me at recess?"

"Sure," Toby replied, more confused than ever. Why, oh, why must he sit alone at lunch?

Toby had only been in the school for a month. He had to change schools when he and his mom had to move into a new house to be closer to his grandparents. His dad was in the Army and serving overseas, so Toby's mom thought it best to be close to her family.

Moving in the middle of the fourth grade wasn't fun for Toby. He had to leave his friends behind and make new ones. He was used to it, though. When his dad was stationed in the States, the family moved a lot.

Toby thought about the other schools he'd attended and how he never ate alone.

Making friends wasn't easy, but Lizzy and Josh seemed to like him. He thought they might want to be his friends someday.

As the class moved outside for recess, Josh ran over to Toby.

"Will you be my friend?" Josh asked.

Toby's eyes lit up, and his heart beat with excitement. "Yes, I'll be your friend."

"It's a deal," Josh said, offering his hand. "Friends, we are!"

"Great," Toby said. "Friends, we are!"

The two tossed a ball, and soon, Lizzy joined them.

They played three-way catch until the bell rang, signaling the time to return to class.

"We'll play again tomorrow," Josh said.

Toby couldn't wait. He had a new friend, and surely, Josh would sit with him at lunch.

He went home smiling from ear to ear. He knew he wouldn't be sitting alone in the cafeteria anymore.

The next day, Toby couldn't wait for lunchtime. He watched the clock, hoping that a lot of time had passed each time he looked.

It seemed to take forever, but finally, the lunch bell rang, and it was time to go to the cafeteria. Toby grabbed his lunchbox from the shelf and stood in line.

As they walked down the hall, Toby's excitement grew. He would soon be at a table with his new friend.

But—that didn't happen. Toby went to his usual seat, and Josh sat at a table with Lizzy and their friends.

Alone again, Toby was confused. He thought of asking Josh but didn't want to seem wimpy. He didn't want to invite himself to their table. They might not like that.

Sad, he faced the reality that his classmates, and even his new friend, didn't want to eat with a black kid.

That has to be it, he thought. *They don't want to eat with me because of my skin color.*

Why were they okay playing with him at recess and touching his hair? Why did Josh ask to be his friend? Don't friends sit together at lunch?

Toby finished his lunch and asked the lunch aide if he could be excused from the cafeteria. Then he went to the nurse's office and asked to lie down.

"What's wrong, Toby?" Nurse Andrews asked.

"My stomach aches," he answered.

Nurse Andrews told him to lie down while she called his mom.

"I'm okay now," he said. "You don't have to call my mom. She'll just worry over a little stomachache."

"Are you sure?" Nurse Andrews asked.

"I'm sure," Toby said. He got up and left.

The rest of the day went slowly, and finally, Toby was home.

"Young man, sit down. I need to speak to you," his mom said, pointing to the living room couch.

"Nurse Andrews called me this afternoon."

"It was just a stomachache, Mom. I ate too fast," Toby said.

"That's not why she called. She wanted to know why I hadn't sent in a doctor's note about your allergies."

Toby looked at his mom, confused. "What allergies?"

His mother gave her son a stern look. "That's exactly my question. Did you tell your teacher you have allergies?"

"No, Mom, why would I do that?"

His mother let out a loud sigh. "Then, why, son, are you sitting at the peanut allergy table in the cafeteria?"

"The what?" Toby asked.

"You heard me—the peanut allergy table in the cafeteria. You don't have peanut allergies. That table is for kids allergic to peanuts who need to sit away from the other kids. Nurse Andrews said you sit there every day and eat alone."

Toby laughed.

"What's so funny, son?"

"Oh, Mom, is that why no one will sit with me at lunch?"

"They can't, Toby. The school has special tables in the cafeteria for different food allergies. The other kids can't sit there because they could have something in their lunches that's harmful to those with food allergies."

Toby stood and danced around the room.

"Mom, I'm so happy! I can't wait to go to school tomorrow."

"Well, you'll have to wait, son."

Toby stopped dancing. "Why?"

"Because tomorrow's Saturday."

Toby laughed and danced his way to his bedroom. He was sure he had found the reason he was sitting alone.

Monday at school, when it was time for lunch, Toby sat at the table with Lizzy and Josh.

"Toby, what are you doing?" Josh asked. "You can't sit here."

"Why not?" Toby asked.

"I've got a peanut butter sandwich, that's why!" Josh shouted. "Do you want to get sick?"

Toby laughed. "I'm not allergic to peanuts or anything else. I didn't know that was the allergy table. Will you still be my friend?"

"Yes, I'll be your friend," Josh said as he scooched over. "Sit right here. It's where you'll sit from now on."

A LITTLE HELP IS ALL YOU NEED

The Weaver Middle School soccer team was on a winning streak. Antonio was giving his all this year, playing his best season yet. He felt happy and satisfied each time the team won, and his teammates would pat him on the back. On the field with his teammates was his favorite place to be.

Off the field, Antonio had different feelings. He did not like school. He especially didn't like homework. He often turned in

42

assignments late or incomplete. He did not see the point in learning all the different subjects when all he wanted was to play soccer.

Coach Canton saw Antonio in the hall between classes and stopped him.

"Hey, Antonio! Bring your lunch to my office today. I need to talk to you about something important. See you at noon."

"No problem, Coach. See you at noon."

Antonio's mind went wild. He imagined all the compliments Coach was going to give him. He imagined Coach talking to him about being team captain next season.

At noon, Antonio carried his lunch tray to the athletics office and knocked on Coach's door.

"Come on in, Antonio. What's for lunch today?" Coach motioned to a small table and two chairs to the right of his desk.

"I got a salad and broccoli. Trying to eat healthily." Antonio hoped this would please Coach.

"Good thinking. Have a seat." Coach sat, taking out his lunch.

"What did you want to talk to me about?" Antonio pushed the broccoli around with his fork.

"Tony, I am so pleased with how you have been playing this season. I can see that you are making a one hundred percent effort on the field. You are applying what I teach you and working well with your teammates. So many others look up to your performance as something to strive toward."

Antonio smiled; his heart felt full.

"But… there is a problem with your performance in the classroom, Tony. Your grades are not as good as they need to be. As a member of the soccer team, you are required to maintain certain grades. And right now, Tony, you do not have those grades." Coach took a bite out of his sandwich and sat back in his chair. Antonio could not remember a time before

44

when Coach had looked at him with disappointment. Antonio didn't like how it felt.

"You must sit out Friday's game. Tony, if your grades do not improve, you cannot continue with the team. It's not the school's rule. The state education department made the rule, and we must abide by it. Your grades need to improve, and fast."

"Coach, I'm sorry. I just...well...I don't like school, and I don't see why I need good grades to play sports."

"I didn't like school much when I was your age, but I loved sports, so I did what I had to do to play," Coach said.

Antonio didn't know what he'd do if he couldn't play. What would he do without his teammates? They were his friends.

He let out a long sigh. "Coach, I will do whatever it takes to stay on the team. I love it so much."

"I know a good tutor who can help you get your grades back on track. His name is Connor. You might know him; his locker is right next to yours."

"Connor Connolly?"

"Yes," Coach answered.

"But he's never said hi to me. Not once. Why would he want to tutor me when he's never spoken a word to me?"

"I've already spoken with him, and he's more than willing to help you with your schoolwork. Think it over, Antonio. I'd hate to lose you on the team."

Coach finished his sandwich. Antonio had lost his appetite and returned his tray to the cafeteria with the salad and the broccoli still on it.

At the end of the day, Antonio stood at his locker, putting his books away. Connor was at his locker, too.

"Hey, Antonio! Coach Canton asked if I could help you with your homework. What day can you meet with me in the library?"

"Why do you want to help me? You've never even said hi to me. Now, you want to help me get my grades up?" Antonio asked, looking Connor in the eyes.

"Hey, I'm sorry," Connor said sincerely. "It's just that you're a sports guy, and from what I've seen, an amazing one, and I'm a geek who no one really likes."

"Why would you say that? Do you think no one likes you? You seem like a cool dude."

"I don't have friends. Have you ever seen anyone hanging at my locker with me?" Connor shrugged his shoulders and closed his locker door. "Let me know what you decide."

"I'll tell you what, Connor. Let's meet in the library tomorrow after school, and you can help me. I have a game on Friday. If you can come, I'll introduce you to my teammates. They are all my friends, and they'll be happy to meet the dude who helps me stay on the team. What do you say?" Antonio asked, hopeful Connor would say yes.

And he did.

The following day, Antonio and Connor sat at the back table in the school library, working on math and science. They were the hardest subjects for Antonio. Somehow, Connor made it easy for Antonio to understand math problems.

"Wow, Connor. You really know how to explain math better than my teacher."

Connor laughed. "It's only because we are one-on-one and not in a room filled with other kids."

Friday came and after the soccer team's big win, Antonio found Connor in the grandstand and brought him to the field to meet the team.

"Hey, Connor, we're all going to Freddie's Restaurant across the street for fries and milkshakes. Can you come with us?" Antonio gave Connor a pleading look.

"Sure... I guess," Connor said. He had never been invited anywhere to be "one of the guys." He tried to hide his excitement.

"Wait here," Antonio said. "I've got to change in the locker room. I'll be right back. Don't go anywhere!"

Antonio's teammates welcomed Connor and invited him to sit with them in the cafeteria at lunch.

Not only did Connor and Antonio become best friends, but Antonio's grades also went up. He was passing everything and allowed to stay on the team.

Antonio got his report card and couldn't wait to show Connor.

"Look at this," Antonio said as they met at their lockers. "You really helped me a lot."

Connor smiled. "You helped me, too. I guess a little help is all we needed."

Antonio high-fived Connor. "Be at my game later."

Connor closed his locker and started walking away. "You bet I will."

ROAD TRIP

Manny looked at the clock. It was noon. He dreaded what was to come.

"Mom, do I have to go?" he whined. "Joey wants me to shoot hoops with him. Can I please do that instead?"

"I'm sorry, Manny. But you need to go with me."

Manny huffed and puffed as he walked to his mother's car. "This isn't fair," he mumbled under his breath. "A sunny Saturday afternoon, and I have to go with my mom."

As his mom drove, Manny sat in the back seat, pouting.

His mother looked at him in the rearview mirror. "You'd better have that look gone by the time we arrive," she said. "You have an hour left to change your attitude."

Manny rolled his eyes and checked his phone. His friends were all doing something fun—but not Manny. No, he had to travel with his mother to visit his grandfather. He hadn't met him before, at least not when he was old enough to remember.

His grandfather lived in California, and Manny and his parents lived in New York. Only a few weeks ago, Manny's grandfather moved to New York, just ninety minutes away. Now that he was so close, they'd be visiting more often, Manny's mother told him. He was not happy to hear that.

It wasn't only the long car ride that bothered Manny; it was missing his Saturday routine of being with his friends. He wanted to play basketball, baseball, or video games with them. Anything was better than visiting with someone he didn't know.

The ride seemed to take forever, and Manny was growing impatient. "Are we almost there, Mom? I mean, the sooner we get there, the sooner we leave, right?"

"We're about five minutes away, and no, we don't get to leave sooner. It doesn't work that way, Manny. This is my father, and I haven't seen him in three years."

"Oh, sorry."

"Someday, you'll understand. The last time I saw my dad was when you and I flew to California to see him. How would you like not seeing me or your father for three years?"

Manny wiggled in his seat. "Sorry, Mom. It's just that I'm eleven. I want to be with kids my age—my friends—and not many grown-ups."

"It will be fine, dear," his mother assured him. "We're here. Now, put a smile on your face, and let's go."

Manny slowly exited the car and walked to the door with his mother. She rang the bell, and an elderly man answered.

Manny watched as they hugged, and his mother cried. He stood back a bit to give them room.

"Oh, Dad," his mother cried. "Here's Emanuel. You haven't seen him since he was five. Look at how he's grown into a young man."

Manny offered his hand to his grandfather but was pulled into a hug. Unsure of what to do, he gave a slight return hug and said, "It's nice to meet you."

As they walked inside, Manny's grandfather said he wanted to hear all about Manny, his friends, and school.

"What would you like to call me?" his grandfather asked. "Grandpa? Elliott?"

"Your name is Elliott?" Manny asked, surprised. "That's such a cool name."

"Is that what you'd like to call me?"

"Sure."

Manny's mother shot a look of disapproval at them both. She didn't like the idea of her son disrespecting her father or any adult. She was raised to be respectful, and she was surprised her father made the offer to a twelve-year-old to refer to him by his first name, but she understood her dad was only trying to make Manny feel comfortable.

"Come to the kitchen," Elliott said. "I've got lunch waiting."

Manny hoped that once they ate, they could be on their way. Wasn't that what people usually did? Eat, talk for a few minutes, then leave? He was anxious to get home before dark to shoot some hoops with Joey. Maybe a game would be going on at the park by the time he got home. That's why Saturdays were so much fun. His mother didn't let him do much on Sundays. She said it was "family day." That's why he didn't understand why they made the trip on Saturday.

"When is Mom arriving?" Manny's mom asked her father.

"She's taking care of selling the rest of the furniture we don't need, then she'll be here. I hope it doesn't take much longer. I miss her being around."

"So do I, Dad."

Manny's mother and Elliott finished eating and sat talking. Elliott saw Manny was bored.

"Say, there, Emanuel, how would you like to come with me to see my special room?"

Manny's mother nodded. "That's a good idea, Dad. Did you get it set up here already?"

"Sure did. Come with me, Manny."

Elliott opened the door to a large room filled with all kinds of telescopes, space suits, and pictures. There was so much to see, Manny's jaw dropped.

"What is all this?" Manny asked as he wandered around the room.

"Manny, did your mother ever tell you what I did for a living?"

"No, why?"

"Have you learned about space in school?"

"Yeah, I have, but I've never looked through a telescope."

"Come spend the night sometime, and I'll show you the universe."

Manny's excitement grew. "I told my mom I want to be an astronaut someday," he said, pointing to a framed photo of an astronaut on a shelf.

"Well, it must run in the family. I'm happy you want to follow in my footsteps."

Manny turned to look at his grandfather. "What do you mean, follow in your footsteps?"

Elliott chuckled. "I'm an astronaut, son. I've been to the moon."

"What?! No way."

"Yes, way."

Manny walked around the room, looking at his grandfather's pictures and memorabilia. Even though his grandfather was young in the photos, he recognized him.

"This is the coolest ever!" Manny said as he stared at a picture of his grandfather as he boarded a spaceship.

"You… you're Elliott Stark! Wow. My class studied you. We learned all about you, and you're my… grandfather!"

Manny was so excited he could barely speak. "Can I… do you think… I would like…"

"What is it, son?"

Manny tried to talk, but no words would come out.

"Let's go back to the kitchen and get you something to drink."

Manny followed his grandfather to the kitchen, where his mother looked through photo albums.

"Mom, you… you never told me."

"I wanted my dad to tell you himself. What do you think?"

"I think it's the coolest. Do you think I could bring Joey the next time we come? Can we come next Saturday? How about tomorrow? It's Sunday. You said Sunday is family day."

"Slow down, Manny. We will be coming often, and you can ask your grandfather about bringing friends here."

"Can I, Grandpa? Can I?"

"Grandpa, hmm. I like the sound of that. Of course, bring all the friends you want. I have plenty of room here. Your grandmother wanted a big house, and she got one. The more, the merrier."

On the ride home, Manny talked nonstop about his grandfather. "How many kids in my school have a grandfather who's been to the moon? It's so cool, Mom."

His mother was happy for Manny, but she wanted to know something.

"Manny, what if Grandpa had been a plumber, accountant, or dentist?"

"He'd still be my grandpa, Mom. That's a silly question. He'd still be cool."

Manny's mother smiled. She wanted to be sure her son loved her father for who he was and not what he was.

"Grandpa is the best," Manny squealed. "He's been to the moon and can make a really good lunch. I can't wait to meet Grandma!"

HELPING HAND

Building a ramp would be difficult, but Milo was determined.
Mrs. Waverly, Milo's neighbor, was generous to those around
her, making baked goods for her neighbors and helping with
their gardens. She had a big smile that rarely left her face. When
Milo was in kindergarten, Mrs. Waverly would help him get on

the bus when his mother had to go to work early in the morning. Each day, she would give Milo cookies to eat after he ate his lunch. She liked to tell stories of her career as an Army nurse, and Milo was fascinated by the tales of the places she had been. But now, Mrs. Waverly was older and had to use a walker to help her walk around. Sometimes, her son had to push her in a wheelchair.

One Sunday, Milo overheard his parents talking about building Mrs. Waverly a ramp so she could get in and out of her house more easily. He knew right away that he wanted to help.

Milo made a list of supplies he'd need and places he would need to go to get them. He told his parents about his plan, and his dad drove him around town to ask for donations.

Milo's first stop was Durk's lumberyard. His dad waited in the car while Mile went inside.

Milo walked over to the counter, where Mr. Durk was standing.

"What can I do for you, young man?" Mr. Durk asked.

"Hello, Mr. Durk. I don't know if you remember me. I'm Milo Stevens. My dad bought lumber from you last spring to build the shed in our backyard."

"I know your dad. I remember you, too. What is it you are looking for today?"

"My neighbor, Mrs. Waverly, has a tough time walking. It is hard for her to climb the stairs on her front porch. I want to build a ramp to make it easier for her, but I need lumber."

"Do you know how to build a ramp, son?" Mr. Durk questioned.

"No, but my dad does, and some of my neighbors," Milo answered nervously.

"Tell me when, where, and how much lumber you need, and I'll deliver it personally," Mr. Durk said, patting Milo on the back. "Have your dad call me with the measurements, and I'll even help you build the ramp."

Milo thanked Mr. Durk and ran to the car, excited to tell his dad.

"Now you have the lumber; what else do you need?"

"Dad, I think I'll need nails and a hammer. Maybe two hammers."

Milo's next stop was Clover Hardware. Destiny Clover had taken over the hardware store from her grandfather, and Milo knew she would be just the person to ask.

Milo burst through the storefront, excited to tell Destiny about his plans. She listened carefully as he explained why building a ramp for Mrs. Waverly was important.

"How could I say no, Milo? This is such a kind thing to do for Mrs. Waverly," Destiny said. "Do you know she used to babysit me? Of course, that was long ago, but I still remember what her house smelled like."

"Blueberry muffins," Milo and Destiny said in unison.

Destiny agreed to donate the hardware and let Milo borrow the tools he needed for the project.

"Thank you so much, Destiny," Milo said as he rushed to the car to tell his dad.

"What else do you need?" his dad asked.

"Nothing I can think of," Milo said.

"Are you sure about that?"

Milo thought for a few minutes as his dad waited for the silence to be broken.

"Son, do you think Mrs. Waverly would want to paint the railings to match the trim on her porch?"

Milo let out a deep breath.

"I almost forgot. We need paint!"

Milo continued his successful streak at the paint store. The owner generously donated a gift card for Mrs. Waverly to buy paint or stain when the ramp was complete.

As he returned home, Milo thought about Mrs. Waverly, her baked goods, and her garden. He was proud of what he had accomplished.

The only thing he needed to do was to find people to help build the ramp. Milo wanted to finish it in a day so Mrs. Waverly could get out if needed.

But how could Milo build a ramp in a day? He'd need a lot of help. He went to bed that night, tossing and turning, thinking of how to get others to help.

Then, like a lightbulb came on, he got an idea.

The next morning, he rushed to get dressed and ran out the door without eating breakfast.

"Milo," his mother called out, "Where are you going in such a hurry?"

"School, Mom. I've got a plan."

Milo huffed and puffed as he walked into the principal's office, catching his breath from his speed running.

"What is it, Milo?" Principal Anderson asked. "You look like a bear has chased you."

"Mr. Anderson, sir, I-I was wondering if I could put posters around the school?" he asked and explained why. "I need volunteers to help build the ramp."

"That's a great idea," Principal Anderson said. "I'll tell you what. I'll ask for volunteers when I make the morning announcements, and I'll stop by with pizza for you all to have for lunch that day."

"Wow," Milo said. "That's so awesome, Mr. Anderson."

"You're awesome," Mr. Anderson said. "You might not know this, but long before you were born, Mrs. Waverly was our school librarian. She was here for many years, even before I came here. You are a fine young man to do this for her."

Milo didn't need to hang any posters. Mr. Anderson's announcement and promise of pizza had volunteers lining up to join in.

Milo could hardly wait to see the smile on Mrs. Waverly's face.

He didn't need to wait long. The following Saturday, everyone showed up at Mrs. Waverly's house. The supplies were unloaded, and the volunteers were ready to get started. Even Mr. Anderson showed up in his work clothes.

They worked all morning, and Mr. Anderson left at noon to pick up the pizzas and juice.

The volunteers sat in the yard, eating and talking about how much they had already done. Mrs. Waverly called to Milo from the window.

"Come here. I have something for you," she said.

Milo walked to the open window, and Mrs. Waverly handed him the biggest plate of chocolate chip cookies he had ever seen."

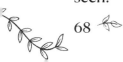

"Thank you, thank you," he said. "They smell so good."

"They are fresh out of the oven," Mrs. Waverly said and winked.

Milo brought the cookies to the volunteers, and they were gone in minutes.

"Back to work," Milo's dad said. "Let's finish up this afternoon."

By five o'clock, the ramp was completed, and Mrs. Waverly stood in her doorway with tears welling in her eyes.

"I don't know what to say. The kindness you've shown me today and every day is overwhelming."

The volunteers clapped and cheered for Mrs. Waverly as she stepped out onto the ramp.

"It's so beautiful," she said. "You are truly remarkable," she said.

As the volunteers cleaned up the tools and prepared to leave, Mr. Anderson made an announcement.

"You students have shown that you will step up and answer the call of duty. Each of you will have a treat waiting in the office Monday morning. You'll all get a voucher to use at the school store."

Mr. Anderson's announcement was greeted with more cheering.

"This has been the best day ever," Milo said as he and his dad walked home.

"It sure was," his dad said. "And tomorrow, Mrs. Waverly's son will be painting the railings. I'm very proud of you, son. You are a fine young man, and you did something Mrs. Waverly will never forget."

"Thanks, Dad. But I just got it started. The rest was teamwork!"

WORKING IT OUT

My name is Manuel. My friends call me Manny. I am twelve years old and live in a town called Bath. It's a funny name, but it's a cool place. On one side of town is a river, and there's a forest on the other side. I live with my parents and annoying little sister on the forest side of town.

I have a best friend named Jordan. We are the same age and height, and he has an annoying little sister, too!

What's awesome is that we have more in common than annoying sisters. We both love to hike in the forest, look for wild mushrooms, identify animal tracks, and dip our feet into the stream to cool off on a hot day. Fishing in the river is another favorite thing of ours. It is a twenty-minute walk to the river, so we make a day of it. We pack lunch and drinks and make sure we have plenty of bait. We have been best friends for two years, and life has been great.

Life is still great. But I have one big problem. Things have changed between Jordan and me. Jordan is distracted and distant. He does not want to explore the forest or go fishing. We do not talk much these days either.

Want to know what changed it all?

Two words.

Cell phone.

Four months ago, we made plans for the spring hiking and fishing season, got our hiking gear in order, made sure our hiking boots still fit, and cleaned our backpacks for another year of exploring and working together to organize our tackle boxes and shovel snow to earn money for new fishing lures.

Then Jordan's parents gave him a cell phone. He was excited, and I was excited for him.

But slowly, the phone became his best friend. Jordan spent less time with me and more time with his phone.

Finally, one day, Jordan invited me to his house for a sleepover. I was happy that we were going to spend time together.

I packed my pajamas and toothbrush in my backpack, and my mom drove me to his house.

"Have a good time," she said when she dropped me off. "Call if you need me for anything."

I got out of the car with my backpack and a bag of snacks Mom made for us. Jordan was waiting for me by the door.

"Get in here," he said. "I can't wait to show you my new game!"

"Oh, we're going to play a game?" I asked. "What kind of game?"

"No, silly. Not you. Me. You can watch. It's a game on my phone. Only one can play."

We walked to his bedroom, and I sat on the edge of the bed next to Jordan.

"Watch this, Manny," he said as the screen jumped from scene to scene. I had no clue what I was supposed to be watching.

"This is kind of boring, Jordan. I have nothing to do."

"What do you mean, boring?" he asked curiously.

"I mean, you invited me here, and you're playing a game. I'm supposed just to sit here and watch?"

"Sure, why not?"

"Because it's boring."

Jordan said nothing and went back to his game. After an hour of doing nothing, I decided to go home. I asked Jordan's mom if she would call my mom to get me.

"Why, honey? Aren't you feeling well?" Jordan's mom asked me.

"I'm okay. It's just that there's nothing for me to do. Jordan's on his cell phone playing a game."

"He is? He's not supposed to be on that phone after five. It's almost seven o'clock. I'm going to have a word with him. Manny, please have a seat in the living room. I'll be back soon."

I waited on the couch in the living room like Jordan's mom told me to do. I just wanted to go home. I thought about leaving and walking home, but Mom wouldn't be too happy with me for walking alone when it was getting dark.

I'd rather be home with my annoying sister than here. If Jordan would rather be on his phone, I guess that's what he should do.

I don't want him to feel forced to do something with me. I wish he never got that stupid phone.

It seemed like forever before Jordan and his mom entered the living room.

"I'm sorry, Manny," Jordan said. "If you want to go home, that's okay."

"Excuse me, Jordan," his mom said. "It's not okay, and we agreed you would stay off the phone for the rest of the night, or I'll take it from you for a week."

"You can't do that, Mom!" You can't take it!" Jordan cried. "Manny can leave."

"Jordan, you invited him over, and now you're saying he can leave? Go to your room, and I'll be there shortly. I want you to think about what you just said."

I watched as Jordan stormed off. "Mrs. Smith, I'd like to go home. Can you please call my mom to pick me up?"

"I will, and I'm so sorry, Manny. I was wrong because I thought Jordan would be more responsible with a cell phone."

Days passed, and I didn't hear anything from Jordan. When I saw him at school, he wouldn't say hi, and he didn't sit with me at lunch like we used to. It didn't matter. Whenever I looked over to the table where he was sitting, he'd have his head down, looking at his phone.

I lost my best friend to a cell phone. I guess it's more fun than I was.

After another day of school without Jordan sitting with me at lunch, telling jokes, and making plans for fishing, I walked into the house to see Jordan's mom sitting at the kitchen table with my mom.

"Manny, Mrs. Smith would like to ask you a few questions," my mom said with a you-will-answer-them look.

I sat down, and Jordan's mom explained that the principal had called her because Jordan was on the phone during social studies class and refused to put it down when the teacher told him to.

"Can you tell me what happened in your own words," Jordan's mom asked.

"I'm sorry, Mrs. Smith. I don't have social studies with Jordan. We are only in lunch and gym together."

"Oh, I see," Jordan's mom looked confused. "I guess then… is there another Manny in your grade?"

"Not that I know of," I answered.

"Jordan told me you asked him to look something up for you on his phone, and that's why he was on it during class."

"Mrs. Smith, Jordan doesn't talk to me anymore since he got the phone. We don't sit in lunch together, and he doesn't say anything to me when I pass him in the hall."

"I-I don't know what to say. It appears Jordan has taken up lying. I need to go now. Thank you, Manny. You've been very helpful."

Wow. Jordan really isn't my best friend. He's not even a friend. He was blaming me when he got into trouble. Friends don't do that to friends.

After dinner, the doorbell rang, and Mom stood at the door talking to whoever it was while I put the dishes in the sink.

"Manny," she called from the living room. "Can you come in here?"

I went in, and Jordan and his mom stood there with Mom.

"Jordan has something to say to you," his mom said. "Go ahead, Jordan."

"I was wrong to be on the phone so much and ignore you. You're my best friend, and you're a lot more fun than a phone," Jordan said with his head down. "I'm sorry I lied about you to Mr. Lee, too."

I wasn't sure what to say.

Jordan lifted his head. "My mom said from now on, we need to solve our problems by talking things out. I know you weren't part of the problem, but I guess problem-solving is better than losing your best friend."

"Where's your phone?" I asked.

"In my mom's purse," he answered. "I can only use it for one hour after school and after I've done my homework. I don't want to use it more than that. I'd rather hang with my bestie."

"Can we hang, Mom?" I asked.

"If Mrs. Smith says it's okay."

Jordan's mom nodded, and my mom led her to the kitchen for pie and coffee.

"Let's go to my room!" I shouted to Jordan. "The last one there is a rotten egg!"

Jordan took off toward my room, laughing. I ran after him as fast as I could, happy we were friends again.

DANCING WITH TWO

LEFT FEET

It was almost time for the Nelson Junior High School's annual

Valentine's dance. It was one of the most exciting times of the

year as the dance was different from most of the school's

dances—the Valentine dance meant girls asked the boys. The

entire school could attend, even the kindergarteners.

The younger kids could ask their dads, brothers, or uncles. The older kids, like Harry, had to be asked by a girl.

And Harry wanted nothing more than to go to the dance with Mandy. He was certain she wouldn't ask him. After all, Mandy was pretty and popular, and Harry was nerdy. Some kids called him "pocket calculator" because he was smart and always at the top of his class.

"No girl will ask me to the Valentine's Day dance," he told his best friend Claude during lunch. "Especially Mandy. She'd never ask me."

"You don't know that, Harry. You need more self-confidence," Claude said.

Harry sighed. "Well, Anna Marie asked you, so you have a date. I'll be the only boy in the school not invited to the dance."

Claude shook his head. "Harry, I can tell Mandy you'd be interested in going with her."

Harry sprang to his feet. "Don't you dare! I would be so embarrassed if you did that. I'll look desperate."

Claude shrugged and sat eating as Harry walked off. He knew it was useless to convince Harry that he was not as unpopular as he thought.

Harry hurried to his locker, hoping he could avoid Mandy. He was worried because Mandy's locker was next to the door to the science room—Harry's next class.

"Hey, Harry!"

Oh, no. The plan to avoid Mandy didn't work. He gave her a nod and rushed into science class.

"How will she ever ask you to the dance if you keep running away from her?" Claude asked as he came up behind Harry.

"She's not going to ask me, and besides, I have two left feet. I can't dance. I look silly when I even try. Why do you think my little sister hasn't asked me to take her? She's going with our dad."

"She probably wants to go with your dad, and I doubt Sally cares how you dance. She's six!"

"Claude, Sally laughed at me all night when I danced at our Uncle Immal's wedding. Then, she teased me when we got home. No, thank you. I am not going to ask anyone to the dance."

"Anna Marie will teach you how to dance," Claude said. "You need to stop making excuses and take some lessons."

Harry took his seat. He wasn't going to take dance lessons, and even if he were the best dancer in the school, Mandy wouldn't go anywhere with the pocket calculator kid.

Harry stopped paying attention to his science teacher and daydreamed about dancing with Mandy. He pictured himself as an amazing dancer who could draw a crowd as he swung his partner around and around.

"Harry… Harry, are you paying attention?" Mr. Southworth asked.

"I, um, well, what's the question?"

The bell saved Harry. He jumped up as it rang and rushed to avoid Mandy.

It didn't work.

"Harry," Mandy called out, "why are you always avoiding me? I don't bite."

Yes, you do, Harry thought, but instead, he turned to her and said, "I can't be late for math."

"Harry Carpenter, you are always avoiding me. I need to ask you something, but you keep running away."

Oh, no. Here it comes. Harry had prepared his answer to decline any invitations to the Valentine's Day dance, and he was about to put it to use.

"What is it?" he asked shyly, ready to give his short speech about how he made plans before he realized it was the same date as the dance.

"Harry, would you… I mean, oh, well, I'll just come right out and ask."

He interrupted, "Mandy, it's okay. You don't need to be scared to ask. The answer is, I'm sorry, but I can't go to the dance with you. I made plans before I knew it was…"

Harry didn't get to finish his sentence because Mandy burst out laughing. "No, silly. I'm not asking you to the dance. I've already asked Michael. Did you really think I'd ask you to go to a dance with me?"

"Well, I—"

"I wanted to ask if you would write a book report for me. I don't want to read the book, and I really need an "A," or my mom and dad will ground me, and I won't be able to go to the dance. I can pay you five dollars."

"Sorry, Mandy. I'm not for sale, and sorry about the mix-up."

Harry rushed off, his face hot and flushed. He wanted to cry. He was so embarrassed. What made him think a girl like Mandy would ask him to the Valentine's dance or any dance?

He saw Claude coming in the opposite direction and tried to speed up so he could duck into the library, but it was too late.

"Dude, what's wrong? You look like you're going to cry, and your face is beet red. You okay?"

"Sure, Claude. I'm fine," Harry answered, his voice cracking.

Claude pulled Harry by the arm. "We're going to talk about this after school. Don't leave without me."

Harry and Claude always walked to and from school together every day. Claude lived two houses away from Harry. They hung out often, and Harry liked Anna Marie even when she interrupted whatever he and Claude were doing.

As they walked home, Harry told Claude everything.

"You're kidding, right? She wanted to pay you to do her homework? A girl like that isn't worth breaking a sweat over. I think you need to forget her. You've crushed on her long enough, and you need to move on."

"She's going to the dance with Michael," Harry said. "She was proud to tell me that."

"Harry, you're going to the dance. I know a friend of Anna Marie's who would love to go with you."

"Who would that be?" Harry asked curiously.

"Demi Fish."

Harry laughed. "Demi Fish? But she can barely speak English."

Claude gave Harry a pat on the back. "Harry, she's a nice girl, and she's been working on her English."

"I'll think about it," Harry said and went inside his house.

He thought Demi Fish was kind of cute, and she smiled a lot, which Harry thought was nice.

After dinner, the doorbell rang. Harry's mom answered.

"Harry, there's someone here to see you," his mother called. "She's in the living room."

She? Who could "she" be? He rushed to the living room to find Mandy sitting with her hands folded in her lap.

"What are you doing here, Mandy? I told you I'm not going to write your book report."

"I know. I came to apologize for asking you to do it and, worse, offering you money. It was wrong, and I'm sorry."

Harry stood, not saying anything but looking Mandy straight in the eyes. "I accept your apology and appreciate that you know it was wrong to ask."

"Thank you, Harry. I was wondering if you'd like to go to the May dance with me?"

Harry was taken by surprise.

"Um, thank you for asking, but no, I have a date. At least, I think I do. Besides, I thought you were going with Michael?"

"I was, but he got the flu."

"I'm not interested in playing second fiddle, but I hope you find a date."

"Thanks, Harry. Again, I'm sorry, and I hope we can be friends." Mandy offered her hand.

"We can be friends," Harry said as they shook. "Come on. I'll walk you out."

Harry said goodbye to Mandy and walked to Claude's house.

"You won't believe this," Harry said. "Mandy came over to apologize and ask me to the dance. I said no, of course."

"Good," a voice from another room called out. "Because I want to ask you."

Demi walked into the room with Anna Marie.

"Demi and Anna Marie are giving me dance lessons," Claude said. "You see, I'm like you. I have two left feet, but that won't keep me from the dance. I don't care what others think of me, and neither should you,"

"Demi, I would love to go with you, but I can't dance at all," Harry said.

"No, no, that's okay. I don't speak English well. So we are… what do you call it? Even?"

Harry laughed. "Even."

The four spent the rest of the evening working on their dance moves. By the night of the dance, Harry was confident he no longer had two left feet.

"Wow, you look beautiful," he said when he picked up Demi to take her to the dance.

As they walked to Harry's mom's car, he gave Claude a thumbs-up. Not only was Harry ready to dance the night away, Demi looked beautiful.

Harry took her hand. "I might not understand everything you say, so please don't get mad, okay?"

Demi smiled. "I won't get mad, Harry. Dancing is a universal language. That is how we can communicate with people all over the world."

Harry couldn't agree more.

CURIOUS CURTIS

Curtis was a curious child. Even when he was a toddler, he explored everything around him. He would pick up bugs and want to know everything about them. When his sister was born, he would look at her for hours, asking his mother questions.

"Why can't she talk?"

"Why does she sleep so much?"

"Why can't she walk?"

"When can she play with me?"

As Curtis got older and started school, he would ask his teachers many questions. Sometimes, his curiosity would cause him to interrupt the lesson to ask something.

When Curtis was in third grade, his teacher, Mrs. McGrath, had no patience with his constant questioning. She sent a note home to Curtis' parents, asking them to teach him better manners so he wasn't interrupting her lessons.

"Please have Curtis understand that I need to teach the entire class and can't be stopping every few minutes to answer his questions," Mrs. McGrath wrote. "He asks questions that are answered as I proceed with the lesson. All he needs to do is wait for me to finish. His questions would then be answered."

Curtis' mother knew of her son's curious nature and inquisitive mind. She had tried everything to get him to stop asking so many questions. She didn't want him to stop completely, but she did want him to slow down at least.

"Curtis, you need to stop interrupting your teachers," his mother told him after reading Mrs. McGrath's note. "You need to let Mrs. McGrath finish her lessons. Then, if you still have questions, you can ask."

"Why?" Curtis asked.

"Why? Because it's not fair to your classmates," his mother answered.

"Why?" Curtis asked again.

"Curtis, we have gone over this many times. You cannot question everything. You need to be respectful of others."

Curtis sighed. "May I go to my room?"

"You may," his mother said. "I will call you when dinner's ready."

Curtis sat at his desk reading an encyclopedia. He liked to read about different people and species of wildlife. When no one would answer his questions, an encyclopedia would. He could let his imagination take him anywhere without his parents' permission. He was happy when he didn't have to ask questions to know more.

Curtis stopped asking so many questions in class; on some days, he didn't ask any questions.

But when he stopped asking questions, his grades started to slide. And that meant another note home from Mrs. McGrath.

"Curtis is no longer interrupting my lessons. In fact, he doesn't seem to pay attention, and his grades are slipping. His English grade has fallen from one hundred to ninety-two, and his reading grade has dropped from ninety-nine to ninety. Although his grades are still high, Curtis is not putting out the quality of work he has been doing. I am concerned his grades will continue to drop without intervention."

Curtis' mom knew she had to do something. Curtis was a smart boy, and he loved school and learning. She didn't understand why he would let his grades slip.

"Curtis, what's going on with you?" she asked him at the dinner table.

"Yes, son, I would like to know, too," his father said.

"Nothing," Curtis answered, not looking up from his plate as he pushed his vegetables around. "Things got harder, that's all."

"Very well," his father said. "We don't expect you always to get perfect grades, but we become concerned when your teacher tells us your grades suddenly dropped."

"Yes, Dad. I'll try to do better," Curtis answered.

"That's all your mother and I expect," his dad said. "Now, how about eating some of those peas instead of pushing them back and forth on your plate."

"Sure, Dad," Curtis answered, taking a spoonful of peas. They were his favorite vegetable.

"Oh, and I almost forgot," his mother said, "your grandfather will pick you up from school tomorrow, and you can spend the weekend with him. Pack what you need tonight, and I'll drop it off to Grandpa after I drop you off at school."

Curtis was excited about spending the weekend with his grandfather. He could ask all the questions he wanted, and his grandfather would answer. No one told him he was interrupting or shouldn't be asking so many questions. He could be himself around his grandpa.

The next morning, Curtis kissed his mother on the cheek and got out of the car. He spent the day not saying anything in class. He did his work, got a perfect score on his math test, and helped a classmate with a science problem. Finally, the bell rang, and Curtis ran to his grandfather's car.

"Let's stop for ice cream," his grandfather said. "Don't you think it's a great day for a large vanilla sprinkle cone?"

"Yes! Curtis was excited. That's one thing he loved about going to his grandfather's. They had ice cream a lot. Curtis knew how much his grandfather loved to eat ice cream, so he never said no. He knew he'd be eating a lot of ice cream all weekend.

When they arrived home from the ice cream stand, Grandpa led Curtis into the house and his den, where he built a hotel model.

"You're the best architect in the world," Curtis said, admiring his model.

Grandpa laughed. "I'm the only architect, you know!"

Curtis asked questions about the hotel, and his grandfather answered each.

Then, Curtis became quiet, and his grandfather asked why.

Curtis explained everything—what his teacher said, the notes home, his slipping grades, and how he can't help but want to know everything there is to know.

"Son, I understand you want to know everything, but the world is large, and it's impossible to know everything. That's why we have careers."

"Careers?" Curtis asked.

"Yes, careers. They are jobs you have for a long time. Take me, for instance. My career is as an architect. Your dad is an accountant. Your mom doesn't work right now, but she was a school principal before you were born."

"I'm sure glad she isn't a school principal anymore. I wouldn't want to be sent to her office!"

Grandpa laughed. "There are plenty of careers for curious boys and girls. Curious people become news reporters, detectives, anthropologists, and geologists. If your curiosity is about animals and how they interact with one another, a

zoologist is a perfect career. You'll find the perfect career for your curious mind when you get older."

"Thank you, Grandpa. Do you mind if I ask you questions about curious careers?"

"Not at all, son. Not at all."

OLIVER'S PERSEVERANCE

Smack! Smack!

A pair of two little feet slapped against the floor.

Delilah sighed as she passed the oil to her mom, "Here he comes…"

The kitchen door swung open.

"I want pizza now!" Oliver exclaimed, frustrated.

Delilah rolled her eyes, and Mom offered a soft smile.

"I'm kneading the dough now, honey," Mom said as she folded and punched the dough. "You know, good things take time."

Oliver's pout deepened. He certainly did not like good things to take time. They did not just take time. They took *too* much time.

He folded his arms across his chest."But waiting is so hard!"

He huffed loudly and stomped out of the kitchen. The pizza took another two hours to reach the dining table. Even though it did taste amazing, Oliver wished it had taken less time.

"Mmmmhhhhh… why did you take so long to get ready," Oliver mumbled as he bit into his slice.

Later that week, Oliver was stuck on a test at school. He looked at his worksheet. Only two out of the ten questions had been answered.

"Ughhhh!" Oliver groaned. It felt like all the numbers were wiggling on the page like ants.

Oliver's brow furrowed. His pencil tapped against the desk.

"Why is this test taking so long?!" he mumbled in frustration.

It wasn't as though Oliver didn't know the test. He had studied for it. He knew how to answer the questions. In his mind, it just took too long to write it all, to solve everything.

Tik, tok, tik, tok.

The time passed quickly.

"That's it!" Oliver said. "I give up!"

He simply could not work his brain harder. It took too long to answer the questions. He picked up his worksheet and stomped to the teacher's desk.

"Are you done?" Ms. Johnson asked as Oliver pushed his test toward her.

She frowned as she unfolded the page and saw eight unanswered questions.

"I'm done," Oliver replied, tapping his foot.

"A good grade doesn't come without hard work, right?" Ms. Johnson pointed out.

"I'm done," Oliver repeated, not looking at his teacher.

He didn't understand adults. Why did they like for things to be slow? Why did they not want everything to happen quickly?

Soon, the bell rang, signalling the end of the school day. Oliver ran and hopped into his mom's car. She was going to take him to his piano class.

"Vroom! Vroom!" The entire way, Oliver imagined he was in a sports car. He sped down the road. A sharp cut and he drifted at the turn. Within seconds, he had reached his destination.

"We're here, Oliver!" his mom announced.

Oliver kissed his mom goodbye and ran to his class. The fleeting time of speeding was gone. Oliver felt he was back in slow motion.

He stood before the piano, its keys gleaming. He played a few notes.

"Ding, ding, ding!"

The music sounded like magic to his ears. Yet, this was all he could do: play random notes. He didn't know how to play an actual song.

Again, there was only one problem. The only problem Oliver had was with everything. Practicing and learning took too much time.

"I'm tired…" Oliver sighed. "I don't have time to practice. I just want to play and make magic happen!"

He had been taking lessons with Mr. Henry for days now. Yet, he couldn't get past the first stanza. Even with that, he made many mistakes. Oliver wished his fingers could create music.

"Oliver, again!" Mr. Henry said sharply. "You know, practice makes perfect."

Oliver sighed deeply. Same old words. Words he did not understand. Yet, he returned his fingers to the piano as Mr. Henry had instructed.

That weekend, the weather was perfect.

"Why don't we go to the beach today?" Oliver's dad asked as he peeked through the curtains early in the morning. And that's how the entire family ended up at the beach.

The sand stretched out as far as Oliver could see. The waves clashed like warriors. Oliver sat to watch this amazing fight. But then, he had another idea. The winning warrior would need a place—a castle, to be exact.

Oliver looked at the sand and the bucket and shovel he had brought. His eyes sparkled with an idea.

Oliver grabbed hold of his toys and started filling the bucket with sand. He pressed the sand into the bucket. He then turned it over to create the base of the castle. He worked hard at it, but suddenly, one side of his castle fell.

"Noooooo!" Oliver cried. He had put so much work into the castle. But now it was ruined.

"I give up…"

Oliver was so angry that he was about to throw his shovel into the sea. That's when he heard another voice.

"Hahahaha!" Oliver looked up to see a girl his age sitting nearby. She was pointing at his ruined castle and laughing loudly. "Awww, you poor baby."

Baby?

Baby!

The word made Oliver angrier than before.

"My castle is perfect." The girl flipped her ponytail proudly.

That was it. The girl had awakened the monster inside Oliver.

"I can make an even better one," Oliver said.

The competition started. Oliver forgot about his first failed attempt and started working on his new castle. His castle did fall many times. Yet, not once did he give up. Oliver had only one thing on his mind. He had to make a castle better than the girl's.

"No," Oliver muttered. "My castle will be better than every kid's castle on this beach!"

Scoop! Pat! Pat!

Oliver worked tirelessly. His hands moved quickly. The sand began to take shape slowly. It grew bigger and bigger.

"Take that!" Oliver grinned, sticking a seashell flag on his castle. He was going to show everyone how great his castle was.

Just as Oliver was about to finish his castle, something happened again. Suddenly, a huge wave crashed into the beach.

SPLASH!!!

Oliver's castle was awfully close to the beach. And so, it was knocked over.

"Ahh!" Oliver shouted but stopped as soon as he saw the girl. Once again, she was laughing at him. Yet, this time, she was joined by another boy. He was trying to make a castle as well.

Seeing their smug faces, Oliver knew only one thing. He was not going to give up. He was going to work even harder. He was going to start over yet again.

"I won't let you guys' win!" Oliver muttered under his breath.

He began building. First, the castle's base and then the walls. Slowly, he put it all together again. It truly was the most giant castle he had ever tried to make.

"I'll show them all!" he thought, filling his bucket with sand.

With a proud smile, Oliver finally finished his sand castle just as his mom walked by.

"Oh my, Oliver!" she said in amazement. "Did you make that?"

"Yes!" Oliver nodded. "I'm in a race."

"Well, I don't know about any race, honey." his mom replied. "But I do see an amazing castle."

"Is it?" Oliver asked, shocked. He looked at his castle again as though for the first time.

"Yes, it's incredible!" his mom replied, excitedly.

Oliver grinned from ear to ear. His castle was bigger than everyone's on the beach. It was also the most beautiful castle he had ever made.

Oliver's mom gathered the entire family to take pictures around his castle. Yet, the whole time Oliver's eyes stayed on his creation. He realized how much time and hard work it took to make the castle fantastic. Yes, there were failures, too. But each failure had taught him something, and each time, he learned how to make his castle even better.

It was the first time in his life he understood the grownups. They were right when they said good things could take time. All he had to do was not give up. And he could do anything he put his mind to.

Things changed from that day. Oliver understood the importance of patience. He knew how important it was to wait for the right time. Yet, while he waited, he also had to work hard for what he wanted and never give up.

In school, Oliver gave proper time to all his tests. He carefully answered all the questions. He knew getting a good grade was not going to be easy.

During his piano lessons, he worked harder. With Mr. Henry, Oliver practiced for hours on end. He recalled how his castle took many tries to build. Just like that, every mistake in his piano lessons helped him get better. And one day, he was going to become the best pianist.

Until then, Oliver was going to keep on working hard. He would never give up because slow and steady wins the race.

EPILOGUE

And I'm back!

You did it. You've reached the end (almost). But a celebration is definitely in order. I'm proud of you!

Between these pages, you went on a journey with your new friends. How fantastic is that? You've learned so much from them. And along the way, you've become even more wonderful.

Remember, just like your new friends, you can do anything. Toby learned to make friends even when it seemed a bit tricky. Antonio found out it's okay to ask for help and get better. Manny understood how all grandparents should be loved and respected. Milo showed how rewarding helping others can be. Manuel thinks smart and solves everything. While Harry finally finds the courage hidden deep inside of him. So, if you are ever

faced with something tough, don't worry! You're a super problem-solver, just like all your new mates.

Remember, keep being the incredible person you are. Spread your magic, just like your friends did in their stories. And you know what? Maybe someday, your own amazing story will be in a book too.

Till then, never forget how special you are. You have made me your fan already. I bet you will make many more.

So, keep being you, dude!

High-fives and fist-bumps,

Michelle

REVIEW

As a children's book author, it would not only be a great help but also a joy for me if you could leave an honest review on Amazon.

I believe that these types of books play a crucial role in nurturing children's character, boosting their self-confidence, enhancing their relationships with friends and family, and encouraging them to be the best version of themselves, all while bringing them happiness.

I hope we can share many more stories together!

Here's the QR code for the review. Choose the marketplace of your preferred country!

| Amazon US review | Amazon UK review | Amazon Canada review |

Printed in Great Britain
by Amazon

34395871R00067